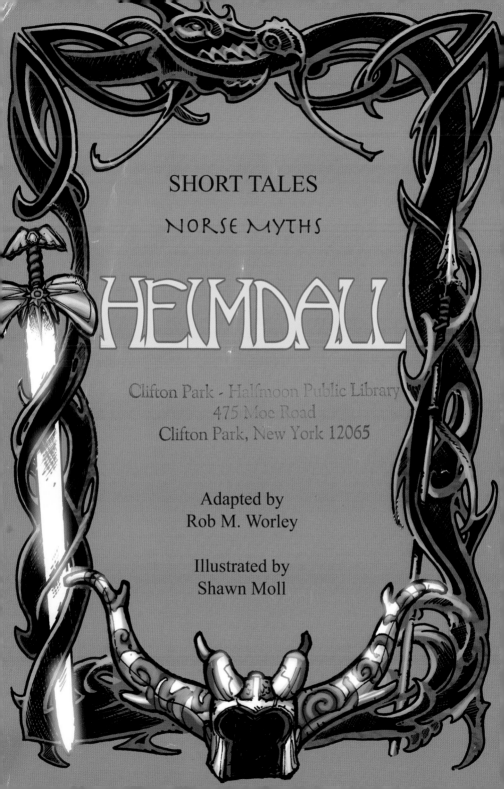

SHORT TALES

NORSE MYTHS

HEIMDALL

Adapted by
Rob M. Worley

Illustrated by
Shawn Moll

visit us at www.abdopublishing.com

Adapted Text by Rob M. Worley
Illustrations by Shawn Moll
Colors by Robby Bevard
Edited by Stephanie Hedlund and Rochelle Baltzer
Interior Layout by Kristen Fitzner Denton
Book Design and Packaging by Shannon Eric Denton

Library of Congress Cataloging-in-Publication Data

Worley, Rob M.
  Heimdall / adapted by Rob M. Worley ; illustrated by Shawn Moll.
    p. cm. -- (Short tales. Norse myths)
  ISBN 978-1-60270-566-1
  1. Heimdall (Norse deity)--Juvenile literature. I. Moll, Shawn. II. Title.
  BL870.H4W67 2009
  398.209363'01--dc22

                                        2008032494

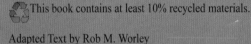

THE NORSE GODS

ODIN:
The All-Father
of the Gods

FRIGGA:
Queen of
the Gods

BALDUR:
The Best Loved
of the Gods

FORSETI:
God of
Justice

HEIMDALL:
The Guardian
of Asgard

HOD:
God of Winter

THOR:
God of Thunder

TYR:
God of War

HERMOD:
Messenger of
the Gods

FREYR:
God of Weather

LOKI:
The Trickster

FREYA:
Goddess of
Beauty and Love

Mythical Beginnings

Heimdall is among the most loved of the Norse gods. He is known by many names, including the Bright God, Gullintani (the golden-toothed), Vindhler (wind shelter), and Riger. Heimdall possessed as many talents as he did names.

Heimdall was given the important task of guarding Asgard, the home of the gods. With his sword, his trumpet, and his horse, Heimdall kept out the Frost Giants.

Heimdall had a most unusual childhood, even for a Norse god. His father was Odin. Odin was the father of all the gods.

Stranger still, Heimdall had nine mothers! They were Gialp, Greip, Egia, Augeia, Ulfrun, Aurigiafa, Sindur, Atla, and Iarnsaxa.

Heimdall's mothers fed him unusual meals. He drank from the sea. He ate the heat of the sun and the strength of the earth! Heimdall was fully grown by the time he was one.

During this time, the gods constructed a rainbow between Earth and Asgard. It was made from fire, air, and water. They called it the Bifrost Bridge.

The gods were quite proud of the bridge. They were also worried.

"What if the Frost Giants use the bridge to enter Asgard?" asked Odin.

The Frost Giants were nasty creatures who wanted to harm the gods.

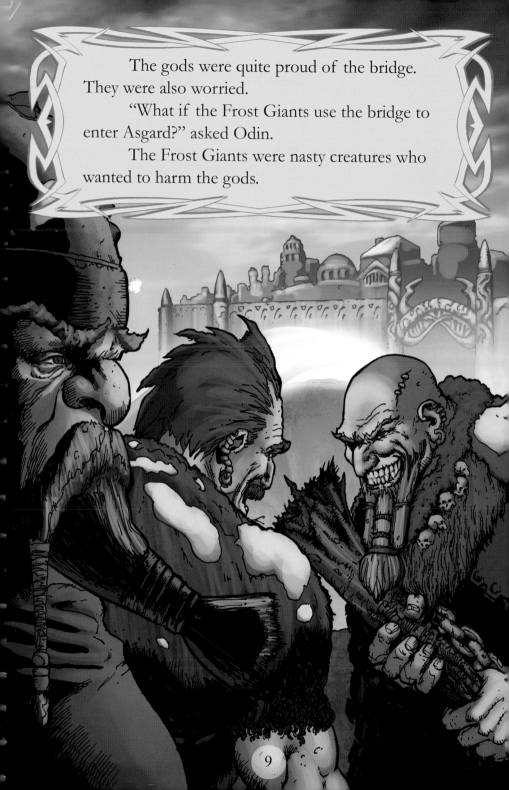

One day, Heimdall found his father worrying about the bridge.

"I can guard the bridge, Father," Heimdall said. "My mothers have raised me to be as strong as any Frost Giant."

"Strength will not be enough," proclaimed Odin. So, the gods granted Heimdall special powers. He could see and hear all parts of the bridge. He also could get a full night's sleep in just a moment's rest.

"Use this mighty sword to drive out any enemies," Odin said. He handed Heimdall a sword that glowed with energy.

"Use this trumpet, Giallar-horn," Odin said. "Bellow with it whenever enemies approach. Its sound will rouse all the creatures of Heaven and Earth."

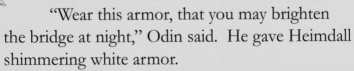

"Wear this armor, that you may brighten the bridge at night," Odin said. He gave Heimdall shimmering white armor.

From that point forward some called Heimdall the Bright God. Others called him the Light God.

"The rainbow bridge is quite long," Odin said. "The mighty steed Gull-top will carry you from end to end."

Each day after that, Heimdall patrolled the bridge. When he was at one end, the Frost Giants would approach the other.

Heimdall would see or hear them from miles away. Gull-top would carry him to them in a blink. Heimdall's bright sword would send them running!

One night, Heimdall heard a strange buzzing noise on the Bifrost Bridge.

The sound came from Asgard. Heimdall looked carefully for the source. Soon he saw a suspicious insect entering the window of the goddess Freya.

Though he was miles away, Heimdall could see that this was no insect. It was Loki, and he had transformed into a fly. The God of Mischief hoped to steal Freya's beautiful necklace.

Loki thought his crime went unnoticed. But Heimdall and Gull-top had seen him. They ran like lightning toward Loki.

"Stop or I'll cut you down, thief!" Heimdall shouted.

Heimdall tried to cut Loki down. But Loki changed into a blue flame. Heimdall's sword passed right through him.

"The gods have granted me great gifts as well," boasted Heimdall. Then, Heimdall became a gush of water. He tried to smother Loki's flame.

But Loki was too quick. He changed into a polar bear. Now, he was large enough to swallow a river.

Heimdall thought of a match just in time. He transformed into a giant grizzly bear. The two bears began to battle.

Heimdall's meals of earth, sea, and sun had made him strong. He was far stronger than Loki. The trickster dropped the necklace and ran away.

"I hope that's the last we'll see of him," Heimdall said to Freya.

"I fear Loki will trouble us for years to come," the goddess said. "One day, you will sound the Giallar-horn for the last time. That day you will stand against Loki in battle."

Many years later, Freya's words came true. Loki returned with his army to destroy all of Asgard.

Heimdall blew his horn and summoned all of the gods into battle. The battle was called Ragnarok. Heimdall and Loki met on the battlefield.

As the flames of Ragnarok died out, a beautiful new world was born. The old gods were gone forever. But the Norse people would always remember the heroic Heimdall, who protected everyone.